This book belongs to

....

make
believe
ideas

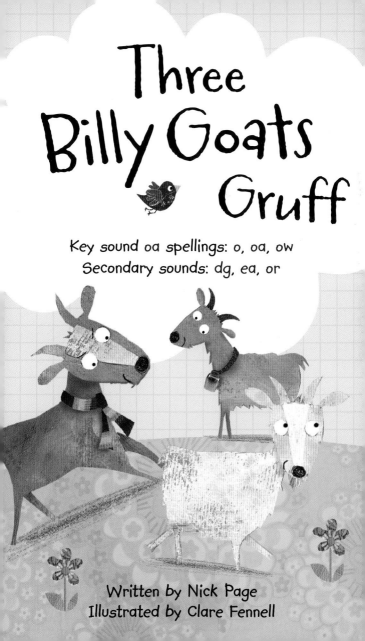

Three Billy Goats Gruff

Key sound oa spellings: o, oa, ow
Secondary sounds: dg, ea, or

Written by Nick Page
Illustrated by Clare Fennell

Reading with phonics

How to use this book

The **Reading with phonics** series helps you to have fun with your child and to support their learning of phonics and reading. It is aimed at children who have learned the letter sounds and are building confidence in their reading.

Each title in the series focuses on a different key sound. The entertaining retelling of the story repeats this sound frequently, and the different spellings for the sound are highlighted in red type. The first activity at the back of the book provides practice in reading and using words that contain this sound. The key sound for **Three Billy Goats Gruff** is oa.

Start by reading the story to your child, asking them to join in with the refrain in bold. Next, encourage them to read the story with you. Give them a hand to decode tricky words.

Now look at the activity pages at the back of the book. These are intended for you and your child to enjoy together. Most are not activities to complete in pencil or pen, but by reading and talking or pointing.

The **Key sound** pages focus on one sound, and on the various different groups of letters that produce that sound. Encourage your child to read the different letter groups and complete the activity, so they become more aware of the variety of spellings there are for the same sound.

The **Letters together** pages look at three pairs or groups of letters and at the sounds they make as they work together. Help your child to read the words and trace the route on the word maps.

Rhyme is used a lot in these retellings. Whatever stage your child has reached in their learning of phonics, it is always good practice for them to listen carefully for sounds and find words that rhyme. The pages on **Rhyming words** take six words from the story and ask children to read and find other words that rhyme with them.

The **Sight words** pages focus on a number of sight words that occur regularly but can nonetheless be challenging. Many of these words are not sounded out following the rules of phonics and the easiest thing is for children to learn them by sight, so that they do not worry about decoding them. These pages encourage children to retell the story, practicing sight words as they do so.

The **Picture dictionary** page asks children to focus closely on nine words from the story. Encourage children to look carefully at each word, cover it with their hand, write it on a separate piece of paper, and finally, check it!

Do not complete all the activities at once – doing one each time you read will ensure that your child continues to enjoy the stories and the time you are spending together. **Have fun!**

By a snowy mountain river,
lived a goat called Little Will.
With him were his bigger brothers,
brother Phil and Big Bad Bill.

Beneath the bridge, across the river,
lived a horrid troll called Sid.
Every day, he croaked a poem,
while below the bridge he hid.

"Beef or pork or lamb to roast,
goat is what I love the most!"

"We should go," said Little Will,
"across the bridge and to the pass,
where the ground is not so frozen,
to a meadow full of grass!"

"I'll go first," said Little Will,
and onto the bridge he ran.
Trip-trap-trip! And from below,
Sid the troll arose and sang . . .

"Beef or pork or lamb to roast,
goat is what I love the most!"

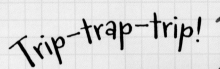

Trip-trap-trip!

"Oh! A goat!" said Sid the troll.
"Just the folk I like to chew.
Since you chose to cross my bridge,
let me sing my song to you.

I like ham and I like chicken,
but what really floats my boat
is the scrummy, finger-licking,
yummy taste of deep-fried goat!"

"Beef or pork or lamb to roast,
goat is what I love the most!"

9

"Don't eat me," says Little Will.
"But if goat is what you prize,
let me over and my bro
will offer you some goat surprise."

"Goat surprise!" says Sid the troll.
"That sounds really quite the thing!"
So Little Will goes to the meadow,
while Sid proceeds to dance and sing,

**"Beef or pork or lamb to roast,
goat is what I love the most!"**

Brother Phil then came on over,
with his great big, shaggy coat.
Trip-trap-trip, onto the bridge,
slowly went this billy goat.

As onto the bridge he ran,
Sid the troll jumped out and sang . . .
"Don't want plums or figs or prunes!
Want some goat upon my spoon!"

"Beef or pork or lamb to roast,
goat is what I love the most!"

"Don't eat me," says Brother Phil.
"I won't fill up your insides.
Let me over and my bro
will offer you some goat surprise."

"Goat surprise!" says Sid the troll.
"Oh, how yummy! Boy, oh, boy!"
Brother Phil goes to the meadow,
while Sid jumps up and down with joy.

14

"Beef or pork or lamb to roast,
goat is what I love the most!"

Trip-trap-trip! And to the bridge,
their great big brother came along.
Massive, huge, with curly horns,
Big Bad Bill was oh-so strong.

As onto the bridge Bill ran,
Sid the troll jumped out and sang . . .
"Don't want onions or shallot,
want some goat here in my pot!"

Beef or pork or lamb to roast,
oat is what I love the most!"

Big Bad Bill says to the troll,
"Pick on someone your own size!
I'm the biggest goat around
and here's my special goat surprise!"

Goat surprise?" cries Sid. "Hooray!
That's what I've been waiting for!
Quick! Don't make me wait all day!
Are there seconds? I want more.

Beef or pork or lamb to roast,
goat is what I love the most!"

Trip-trap-trip went Big Bad Bill,
and with a cry of "Tally-ho!",
he charged toward the troll so fast,
he hit him like a hammer blow.

Sid was thrown into the heavens,
floated through the wintry skies!
As he rose, they heard him wailing,
"I don't like this goat surprise!"

Oh!

"Beef or pork or lamb to roast,
goat is what I love the most!"

21

Those three goats now have their home
in the meadow on the hill.
If you go there, say "hello" to
Will and Phil and Big Bad Bill.

Where is Sid? Well, no one knows,
he went away and wrote a note,
chose to give up eating meat,
said, "I've really gone off goat!"

"Beef or pork or lamb to roast,
goat is what I hate the most!"

23

Key sound

There are several different groups of letters that make the **oa** sound. Read the words and tell the troll which plate contains his food.

flow

blow

know

throw

below

snow

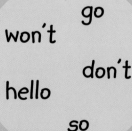

go

won't

don't

hello

so

boat

load

toad

coat

road

goat

float

note

wrote

home

rose

close

over

Letters together

Look at these pairs of letters and say
the sounds they make.

dg **ea** **or**

Follow the words that contain **dg** to
find a bridge for the goat to cross.

dg

waves

badge   sludge

fudge   lost

rich   judge

bridge   catch

right

What do you want to eat? Follow the words that contain **ea** to find a peach.

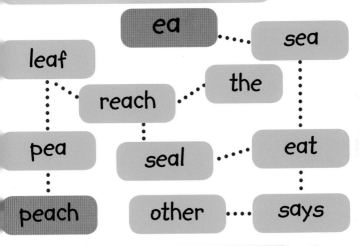

ea · · · · sea

leaf

the

reach

pea

seal

eat

peach

other · · · · says

Follow the words that contain **or** to find some pork for Sid's dinner.

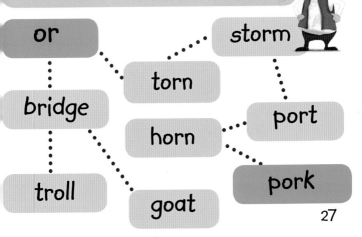

or

storm

torn

bridge

port

horn

troll

goat

pork

Rhyming words

Read the words in the flowers and point to other words that rhyme with them.

| gruff | **me** | we |
| fork | | she |

| glass | **pass** | beef |
| here | | grass |

| ill | **hill** | till |
| ran | | sang |

three	**pork**	snowy
fork		cork

boat	**goat**	ground
coat		troll

meadow	**dance**	chance
prance		bridge

Now choose a word and make up a rhyming chant!

A **goat** in a **coat** on a **boat** with a sore **throat**!

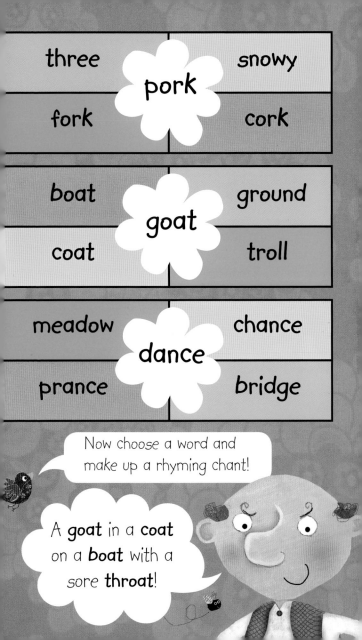

Sight words

Many common words can be difficult to sound out. Practice them by reading these sentences about the story. Now make more sentences using other sight words from around the border.

Big Bad said, "I'm biggest around

Sid wanted to eat the **three** billy goats.

The goats wanted to live **where** the ground was not frozen.

Nobody saw the troll again.

saw · put · of

· here · by · could · three · a · make · came · your

The goats ran **over** the bridge.

"Don't eat me," **said** Little Will.

Sid the troll lived **under** the bridge.

Sid didn't try to eat Little Will **or** Phil.

The goats made the meadow their **home**.

Sid went **away**.

or • who • there • good • how • under • said • I'll • where • going • home • over • did

so • made • think • here • about • away • ran • want •

Picture dictionary

Look carefully at the pictures and the words.
Now cover the words, one at a time.
Can you remember how to write them?

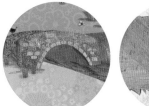

bridge

coat

goat

grass

horns

meadow

river

snowy

troll